Dear Parent:

Congratulations! Your child is taking the first steps on an exciting journey. The destination? Independent reading!

STEP INTO READING® will help your child get there. The program offers five steps to reading success. Each step includes fun stories and colorful art. There are also Step into Reading Sticker Books, Step into Reading Math Readers, Step into Reading Write-In Readers, Step into Reading Phonics Readers, and Step into Reading Phonics First Steps! Boxed Sets—a complete literacy program with something for every child.

Learning to Read, Step by Step!

Ready to Read   Preschool–Kindergarten
• big type and easy words • rhyme and rhythm • picture clues
For children who know the alphabet and are eager to begin reading.

Reading with Help   Preschool–Grade 1
• basic vocabulary • short sentences • simple stories
For children who recognize familiar words and sound out new words with help.

Reading on Your Own   Grades 1–3
• engaging characters • easy-to-follow plots • popular topics
For children who are ready to read on their own.

Reading Paragraphs   Grades 2–3
• challenging vocabulary • short paragraphs • exciting stories
For newly independent readers who read simple sentences with confidence.

Ready for Chapters   Grades 2–4
• chapters • longer paragraphs • full-color art
For children who want to take the plunge into chapter books but still like colorful pictures.

STEP INTO READING® is designed to give every child a successful reading experience. The grade levels are only guides. Children can progress through the steps at their own speed, developing confidence in their reading, no matter what their grade.

Remember, a lifetime love of reading starts with a single step!

For Peter, Laura, and Billy,
who always want a hug!
—A.S.C.

Text copyright © 2000 by Alyssa Satin Capucilli. Illustrations copyright © 2000 by Jim Ishi.
All rights reserved under International and Pan-American Copyright Conventions. Published in
the United States by Random House Children's Books, a division of Random House, Inc., New
York, and simultaneously in Canada by Random House of Canada Limited, Toronto. Originally
published by Golden Books, an imprint of Random House Children's Books, a division of
Random House, Inc., in 2000.

www.stepintoreading.com

Educators and librarians, for a variety of teaching tools, visit us at
www.randomhouse.com/teachers

Library of Congress Cataloging-in-Publication Data
Capucilli, Alyssa Satin, 1957–
Bear hugs / by Alyssa Satin Capucilli ; illustrated by Jim Ishi. — 1st Random House ed.
  p.   cm. — (Step into reading. A step 1 book)
SUMMARY: Baby Bear decides that of all the hugs from Mama and Papa Bear, a group hug
is best.
ISBN 0-307-26113-1 (pbk.) — ISBN 0-307-46113-0 (lib. bdg.)
[1. Hugging—Fiction. 2. Bears—Fiction.]
I. Ishi, Jim, ill.   II. Title.   III. Series: Step into reading. Step 1 book.   PZ7.C179Be   2003
[E]—dc21   2002012965

Printed in the United States of America   18 17 16 15 14 13
First Random House Edition
STEP INTO READING, RANDOM HOUSE, and the Random House colophon are registered trademarks
of Random House, Inc.

Bear Hugs

by Alyssa Satin Capucilli
illustrated by Jim Ishi

Random House 🏠 New York

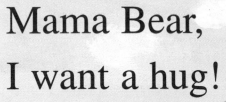

Mama Bear,
I want a hug!

A big hug?

A small hug?

A growing very tall hug?

Papa Bear,
I want a hug!

A wet hug?

A dry hug?

A fly up to the sky hug?

How about a funny hug?

How about a honey hug?

A blackberry hug?

A blueberry hug?

A nose all red
with cherry hug?

How about a wiggly hug?

How about a giggly hug?

WAIT!

I know the hug
that's best for me.

It's a hug—
a hug for three!